FUNNY JOKES

FOR

12

YEAR OLD KIDS

HUNDREDS OF HILARIOUS JOKES INSIDE!

JIMMY JONES

Hundreds of really funny, hilarious jokes that will have the kids in fits of laughter in no time!

They're all in here - the funniest
- Jokes
- Riddles
- Tongue Twisters
- Knock Knock Jokes

for 12 year old kids!

Funny kids love funny jokes and this brand new collection of original and classic jokes promises hours of fun for the whole family!

Books by Jimmy Jones

Funny Jokes For Funny Kids
Knock Knock Jokes For Funny Kids

Funny Jokes For Kids Series
All Ages 5 -12!

To see all the latest books by
Jimmy Jones just go to
kidsjokebooks.com

Contents

Funny Jokes!

Why did the monkey have a day off?
Work was driving him bananas!

Which channel did cavemen watch?
The Pre-History Channel!

Why can't you see elephants hiding in a tree?
Because they are really good at it!

What did the doctor say to the patient who snored so much he woke himself up?

Try sleeping in the other room!

Why did the restaurant on the moon close?

It had no atmosphere!

What did Kermit the Frog and Alexander the Great have in common?

The same middle name!

Why couldn't the cross eyed teacher get a job?

She couldn't control her pupils!

Why was the oyster sad when she left the gym?

She pulled a mussel!

What happens if you feed gun powder to chickens?

Egg-splosions!

What did the leopard say after lunch?

That really hit the spots!

What do you have if you get scared by the same ghost twice?

Deja boo!

Why did the pirate get his new ship so cheaply?

It was on sail!

What did the doctor say to the patient who was sick for the first 30 minutes every morning?

Get up half an hour later!

What do you call a lion that likes to wear top hats?

A dandy lion!

What did the doctor say when the nurse lost the scales?

No weigh!

What did the thief get after he stole a calendar?

12 months!

What do Cannibals call athletes?

Fast Food!

What was the boy always late for school?

They kept ringing the bell before he got there!

What do birds send out at Halloween?
Tweets!

Why did the hummingbird always hum?
She forgot the words!

Why did the teacher turn off the lights?
The students were too bright!

Where do dogs go if they lose their tails?
A re-tail shop!

What did the sad nose say to his mom?
Everyone is picking on me!

Why do violins exercise so much?
To be as fit as a fiddle!

Why did the cat swim?
She was a platy-puss!

What fish would never bite a woman?
A man eating shark!

How did the frog feel when she hurt her leg?
Un-hoppy!

What do vegan zombies eat for lunch?
A bowl of graaaaaaaains!

Who hid in the bakery on Christmas Eve?
The mince spy!

Why did the toilet go to hospital?
It was feeling flushed!

Why did the woodcutter chop off the wrong branch?

It was an axe-ident!

Why couldn't the aliens get a park on the moon?

It was full!

What is even better than a talking dog?

A spelling bee!

Why was Mickey Mouse in trouble at school?

He was being too Goofy!

Why was the cucumber sad?

She was in a pickle!

What did Mrs Claus say to Santa Claus when she looked out the window?

It looks like rain, dear!

Why did the gorilla have huge nostrils?
She had big fingers!

Why didn't the girl join the track team?
There were too many hurdles!

Who wrote the famous book 'Salty Fish'?
Anne Chovie!

What shoes do chickens wear to the gym?
Re bok bok boks!

How much does it cost when a pirate gets his ears pierced?
About a Buccaneer! (A buck an ear)

What did the dog wear to chemistry class?
A lab coat!

Which vegetable gets served in jail?

Cell-ery!

When the boy stayed up all night thinking about where the sun went, what happened next?

It finally dawned on him!

What did the bees do when they moved into their new house?

They had a house swarming party!

Why did the cow go to yoga class?
To be more flexi-bull!

What happens if a dog eats way too much garlic?
His bark is worse than his bite!

What did the hedgehog say to the cactus?
Hi dad!

What do you do if a monster rolls his eyes
at you?

Roll them back to him!

What do you call a dog with a sore throat?

A husky!

What happened to the man who got cut in
half and lost his entire left side?

He's all-right now!

Why did the judge sentence the fish to 3 years in jail?

He was Gill Ty!

What did the baker do when she won the lottery?

She kept all the dough!

What did the surgeon do to the patient who had water on the brain?

Gave him a tap on the head!

What is black, white and pink?
An embarrassed penguin!

Why did the comet go to Hollywood?
She wanted to become a star!

What do you call two guys with no arms or legs hanging above the window?
Curt and Rod! (Curtain Rod!)

What do you call a lying snowman?
A snow fake!

What did the doctor say to the patient who told him he broke his leg in 2 places?
Stop going to those places!

If you are really cold and grumpy what do you eat?
A brrrgrrr!

What did the rude young dinosaur call his granddad?

An old fossil!

Where is the witch's garage?

The broom closet!

Why are triangles good at playing basketball?

They get three pointers!

Which cell phones taste yummy?
Blackberries!

Why didn't the shark eat the man in the submarine?
He didn't like canned food!

What do you get if an elephant stands on the roof of your house?
Mushed rooms!

What did the policeman say to the robber snowman?

Freeze!

Which superhero has a part time job pressing shirts?

Iron Man!

Why did everyone trust the caveman?

He was a caveman of his word!

What is a pig called if she can write with both hooves?

Ham-bidextrous!

What did the doctor say to the boy who thought he was a werewolf?

I think you just need to comb your face!

What can make an octopus giggle?

Ten tickles! (tentacles)

Why did the toilet paper roll down the steep hill?

He wanted to get to the bottom!

What do you get if you cross a robber with a concrete mixer?

A hardened criminal!

Why was the beach wet?

The sea weed!

What did the big steak say to the little steak?

So! We meat again!

What did the sad banjo say to her mom?

Everyone keeps on picking on me!

What did one tomato say to the other tomato in the tomato race?

Ketchup!

What was the fly doing in the bowl of soup?
Backstroke!

Why do mice take really long showers?
They like to feel squeaky clean!

What exercise do cats do in the morning?
Puss Ups!

Which dinosaur lifted heavy weights at the gym?

The Tyrannosaurus Pecs!

What do you call an insect who can't speak clearly?

A mumble bee!

How did the swim team get to practice?

They carpooled!

What did the boxer drink just before the big fight?

Fruit punch!

What did the cannibal say when he saw 2 campers in their sleeping bags?

Breakfast in bed!

What did the doctor do to the patient who thought he was a duck?

Gave him a clean bill of health!

Funny Knock Knock Jokes!

Knock knock.

Who's there?

Wheel.

Wheel who?

Wheel need to hurry to get there on time!

Knock knock.

Who's there?

Razor.

Razor who?

Razor hands, this is a stick up!

Knock knock.

Who's there?

Carmen.

Carmen who?

Carmen get your hotdogs!

Fresh hotdogs for sale!

Knock knock.

Who's there?

Noah.

Noah who?

Noah good place for lunch?

How about pizza?

Knock knock.

Who's there?

Daisy.

Daisy who?

Daisy me running but 'dey can't catch me!

Knock knock.

Who's there?

Area.

Area who?

Area deaf!

I've been knocking for 2 days!

Knock knock.

Who's there?

Alaska.

Alaska who?

Alaska you one more time!

Please open the door!

Knock knock.

Who's there?

Yacht.

Yacht who?

Yacht to be able to recognize me.

I only saw you last week!

Knock knock.

Who's there?

Fortification.

Fortification who?

Fortification we are going to Florida!

Knock knock.

Who's there?

Amanda.

Amanda who?

Amanda repair that window you broke wants to charge me $300!

Knock knock.

Who's there?

Henrietta.

Henrietta who?

Henrietta apple and he found half a worm!

Knock knock.

Who's there?

Amish.

Amish who?

You're not a shoe, you're a person!

Knock knock.

Who's there?

King Tut.

King Tut who?

King Tut key fried chicken for dinner tonight!

Knock knock.

Who's there?

Isabel.

Isabel who?

I know there Isabel but I like knocking!

Knock knock.

Who's there?

Furry.

Furry who?

Furry's a jolly good fellow!

Knock knock.

Who's there?

Owls say.

Owls say who?

Yes they do!

You are now an Owl expert!

Knock knock.

Who's there?

Dozen.

Dozen who?

Dozen anybody want to let me in?

It's cold out here!

Knock knock.

Who's there?

Miniature.

Miniature who?

Miniature let me in I'll pay you that

money I owe you!

Knock knock.

Who's there?

Nanna.

Nanna who?

Nanna your business! It's top secret!

Knock knock.

Who's there?

Bud.

Bud who?

Bud I really want to know - where is the doorbell?

Knock knock.

Who's there?

Tish.

Tish who?

No thanks. I use a handkerchief!

Knock knock.

Who's there?

Philip.

Philip who?

Philip up the pool so we can have a swim! It's so hot!

Knock knock.

Who's there?

Theodore.

Theodore who?

Theodore seems to be really hard to open! Is it stuck?

Knock knock.

Who's there?

Sweet Tea.

Sweet Tea who?

Please be a Sweet Tea and open the door!

Knock knock.

Who's there?

Panther.

Panther who?

My Panther falling down!

Help!

Knock knock.

Who's there?

Arfur.

Arfur who?

Arfur got why I came over!

Knock knock.

Who's there?

Cash.

Cash who?

You sound like you are a little bit nutty!

Knock knock.

Who's there?

Mouse.

Mouse who?

Mouse is getting painted today so can I come in please?

Knock knock.

Who's there?

Otto.

Otto who?

Otto know but I can't remember!

Knock knock.

Who's there?

Gopher.

Gopher who?

I could Gopher a milkshake right now!

Knock knock.

Who's there?

Jupiter.

Jupiter who?

Jupiter invite in my letterbox?

It looks like your writing.

Knock knock.

Who's there?

Nun.

Nun who?

Nun of your business my good sir!

Knock knock.

Who's there?

Wafer.

Wafer who?

I've been a Wafer so long I forgot where you live!

Knock knock.

Who's there?

Fanny.

Fanny who?

Fanny body knocks just pretend you're not home!

Knock knock.

Who's there?

Sarah.

Sarah who?

Is Sarah tall person here who can reach this doorbell?

Knock knock.

Who's there?

Tick.

Tick who?

Tick 'em up! I'm a wobber!

Knock knock.

Who's there?

Pop.

Pop who?

Pop on over to my place.

We're having ice cream!

Knock knock.

Who's there?

Walter.

Walter who?

Walter you doing for lunch?

I'm sooooo hungry!

Knock knock.

Who's there?

Dumbbell.

Dumbbell who?

Dumbbell needs to be fixed so I don't have to knock!

Knock knock.

Who's there?

Norma Lee.

Norma Lee who?

Norma Lee I wouldn't knock but I forgot my key!

Knock knock.

Who's there?

Wilfred.

Wilfred who?

Wilfred be able to come out to play?

Knock knock.

Who's there?

Flea.

Flea who?

I knocked Flea times!

Why didn't you answer?

Knock knock.

Who's there?

Detail.

Detail who?

Detail of your cat is so fluffy I want to tickle your chin with it!

Knock knock.

Who's there?

Sherwood.

Sherwood who?

Sherwood would like to come in before it gets dark!

Knock knock.

Who's there?

Mikey.

Mikey who?

Mikey is too big for the keyhole!

Noooooo!

Knock knock.

Who's there?

Norway.

Norway who?

Norway am I leaving until you tell

me the truth!

Knock knock.

Who's there?

Poor me.

Poor me who?

Poor me a glass of water!

I'm really thirsty!

Knock knock.

Who's there?

Sister.

Sister who?

Sister right place for the party

tonight?

Knock knock.

Who's there?

Scott.

Scott who?

Scott nothing to do with you!

Knock knock.

Who's there?

Orson.

Orson who?

Orson cart will get us to school!

Let's go!

Knock knock.

Who's there?

Sawyer.

Sawyer who?

Sawyer were home.

Where have you been all these years?

Knock knock.

Who's there?

Avon.

Avon who?

Avon you to open ze door!

Knock knock.

Who's there?

Luke.

Luke who?

Luke through the window and find out!

Knock knock.

Who's there?

Augusta.

Augusta who?

Augusta wind nearly blew me over!

Knock knock.

Who's there?

Seymour.

Seymour who?

I Seymour when I wear my glasses!

Knock knock.

Who's there?

Gerald.

Gerald who?

It's Gerald friend from school!

Don't you recognize me?

Knock knock.

Who's there?

Hamish.

Hamish who?

Hamish you so much when I don't see you!

Knock knock.

Who's there?

Ammonia.

Ammonia who?

Ammonia short person so I can't reach the bell!

Knock knock.

Who's there?

Father.

Father who?

Father last time please open the door before I starve!

Knock knock.

Who's there?

Tahiti.

Tahiti who?

Tahiti home run you need to hit the ball really hard!

Funny Riddles!

Which bird is always welcome when you are eating?

A swallow!

I'm tall when I'm young but short when I'm old. What am I?

A candle!

Which snake is good at math?

The Pi-thon!

What has a head and a tail but no arms?
A coin!

Which fruit is in every diary?
Dates!

How much dirt is in a 3 feet deep by 4 feet wide by 6 feet long hole?
None. It's a hole!

How can you cure lockjaw?
Swallow a key!

People buy me to eat and never eat me.
What am I?
A fork!

What has hands but cannot clap?
A clock!

Which 5 letter word sounds the same if you take away its first or middle letter?
EMPTY!

Why is a bus driver like a plant?
They both have routes!

What do you call a wooden shoe in the sink?
A clogged drain!

What kind of room has no windows or doors?

A mushroom!

What has one eye but cannot see?

A needle!

What can you draw without a pencil?

The blinds!

What is thin, can bend, is red on the inside
with a nail on the end?

A finger!

What can clap but has no hands?

Thunder!

What can you measure even though
sometimes it flies?

Time!

Why can't frogs die from a really sore throat?

They can't croak!

How can a pocket be empty but still have something in it?

If it has a hole in it!

Which bee will never sting you?

A frisbee!

What do you always break before you can use it?

An egg!

What has feathers but no wings?

A pillow!

What can run but never walks?

A river!

Why do giraffes have such long necks?
They have very smelly feet!

What can run but never walk?
A tap!

What is the most curious letter?
Y!

What is always coming but never arrives?
Tomorrow!

Why are eggs never funny?
They tell bad yokes!

What allows you to look straight through walls?
A window!

What is it called when someone steals your cup of coffee?

A mugging!

What key do you get at Christmas?

A turkey!

What do you call a shape that has vanished?

An octo-gone!

You can see me in water but I am never wet. What am I?

Your reflection!

What should you do if you get a rash from biting insects?

Stop biting insects!

What has a neck but no head?

A bottle!

Funny Tongue Twisters!

Tongue Twisters are great fun!
Start off slow.
How fast can you go?

Three free fleas flew.
Three free fleas flew.
Three free fleas flew.

Willy's real rear wheel.
Willy's real rear wheel.
Willy's real rear wheel.

Unique New York.
Unique New York.
Unique New York.

Bill blew blue bubbles.
Bill blew blue bubbles.
Bill blew blue bubbles.

Tie twine to three tree twigs.
Tie twine to three tree twigs.
Tie twine to three tree twigs.

Creepy crabs clammer.
Creepy crabs clammer.
Creepy crabs clammer.

Clean clam can.
Clean clam can.
Clean clam can.

Four furious friends fly forward.
Four furious friends fly forward.
Four furious friends fly forward.

Silly sheep weep and sleep.
Silly sheep weep and sleep.
Silly sheep weep and sleep.

Which wrist watch?
Which wrist watch?
Which wrist watch?

Three short sword sheaths.
Three short sword sheaths.
Three short sword sheaths.

Five free frogs.
Five free frogs.
Five free frogs.

She saw seashells on the seashore.
She saw seashells on the seashore.
She saw seashells on the seashore.

Butter bucket bottom.
Butter bucket bottom.
Butter bucket bottom.

Green glass globes glow greenly.
Green glass globes glow greenly.
Green glass globes glow greenly.

Rough rafting rapids.
Rough rafting rapids.
Rough rafting rapids.

Six shoe shine.
Six shoe shine.
Six shoe shine.

Sammy's short suit shrunk.
Sammy's short suit shrunk.
Sammy's short suit shrunk.

She flosses fast.
She flosses fast.
She flosses fast.

The fish shop sells shellfish.
The fish shop sells shellfish.
The fish shop sells shellfish.

Seven slimy snakes.
Seven slimy snakes.
Seven slimy snakes.

Crisp crusts crackle.
Crisp crusts crackle.
Crisp crusts crackle.

Six thick sticks.
Six thick sticks.
Six thick sticks.

Bonus Funny Jokes!

How do divers sleep under the sea?
They use a snore-kel!

What did the astronaut drink on his break?
A nice cup of gravi-tea!

What was the apple doing at the gym?
Working on her core!

Why did the skeleton fail the test?
He was a numbskull!

Why couldn't the girl sell a joke book at school?
New school policy -no funny business!

Where did the pencil go for his vacation?
Pencil Vania!

What would you call it if worms took over the entire world?

Global Worming!

Why do hard boiled eggs always win at cards?

They are hard to beat!

Where did the shark post his photos?

Finstagram!

What do you call a dinosaur who is a loud sleeper?

A Bronto-snorus!

What is a good dessert for a ghost?

I Scream and Booberry pie!

Why do sea turtles watch the news?

To keep up with current events!

Why didn't the bear wear shoes to school?
He liked to have bear feet!

What do you call a snowman on a skateboard?
A snow mobile!

What do Eskimos use to fix their house?
Ig-glue!

What do you call a crazy loaf of bread.
A weir-dough!

Why was the librarian feeling stressed?
She was overbooked!

Why did the boy lay down in the fireplace?
He wanted to sleep like a log!

Where do skeletons go to jail?
The rib cage!

Why did the meteorologist have a day off?
He was a bit under the weather!

Why was the ocean so upset?
It had crabs on its bottom!

What was a better invention than the first telephone?

The second telephone!

If a boomerang doesn't come back, what is it?

A stick!

What do you call an ugly dinosaur?

An Eye-saur!

Why wouldn't the baby blueberry stop crying?

Her dad was in a jam!

What was the boy eating while having a bath?

Sponge cake!

What side of a bird has the most feathers?

The outside!

How can you get rich by eating?
Just eat Fortune Cookies!

What should you eat if you have a cold?
Maccaroni and Sneeze!

Why did the elephant decide to leave the circus?
He was sick and tired of working for peanuts!

What did the teenage dinosaur think when he lost his cell phone?

His social life was extinct!

Which dinosaur just broke up with his girlfriend?

The Tyrannosaurus Ex!

Why did the whale blush?

She saw the ocean's bottom!

Why was the broom late for work at the factory?

He overswept!

Why did the gorilla wear a suit?

To do some monkey business!

What do you call a boy with lots of vegetables in your hot tub?

Stew!

Bonus

Knock Knock Jokes!

Knock knock.

Who's there?

Safari.

Safari who?

Safari so goody!

Knock knock.

Who's there?

Cook.

Cook who?

Are you a cuckoo clock?

Knock knock.

Who's there?

Vitamin.

Vitamin who?

Vitamin for the party!

He's a lot of fun!

Knock knock.

Who's there?

Major.

Major who?

Major day with all these jokes, didn't

I?

Knock knock.

Who's there?

Howard.

Howard who?

Howard you like to go to the park and play ball?

Knock knock.

Who's there?

Ash.

Ash who?

Bless you! Would you like a tissue?

Knock knock.

Who's there?

Quiet Tina.

Quiet Tina who?

Quiet Tina Library!

I'm trying to read!

Knock knock.

Who's there?

Disguise.

Disguise who?

Disguise the limit!

Knock knock.

Who's there?

Roxanne.

Roxanne who?

Roxanne pebbles make a really nice rock garden!

Knock knock.

Who's there?

Wanda.

Wanda who?

I Wanda what Billy's up to today?

Let's go ask him!

Knock knock.

Who's there?

Armageddon.

Armageddon who?

Armageddon outta here!

Knock knock.

Who's there?

Ben.

Ben who?

Ben away for years but now I'm back!

Let's party!!

Knock knock.

Who's there?

Carrie.

Carrie who?

Carrie on old chap!

Knock knock.

Who's there?

House.

House who?

House about we go to the mall?

Let's go!

Knock knock.

Who's there?

Oscar.

Oscar who?

Oscar locksmith to open this door if you lost your key!

Knock knock.

Who's there?

Dishes.

Dishes who?

Dishes the police!

Open up!

Knock knock.

Who's there?

Jamaica.

Jamaica who?

Jamaica mistake? You forgot to leave the key under the mat!

Knock knock.

Who's there?

Shemp.

Shemp who?

Shempoo your hair please, it looks dirty!

Knock knock.

Who's there?

Lucy.

Lucy who?

Lucy lastic and your pants fall down!

Knock knock.

Who's there?

Voodoo.

Voodoo who?

Voodoo you think you are, making me wait so long!

Knock knock.

Who's there?

Sid.

Sid who?

Sid you would be ready by now!

Why are you late?

Knock knock.

Who's there?

Hammond.

Hammond who?

Hammond eggs on toast!

Yummy!

Knock knock.

Who's there?

Pudding.

Pudding who?

I'm pudding on my best dress for dinner! Do you like it?

Knock knock.

Who's there?

Myth.

Myth who?

I myth you tho much!

Where have you been all these years?

Thank you so much

For reading our book.

I hope you have enjoyed these funny jokes for 12 year old kids as much as my kids and I did as we were putting this book together.

We really had a lot of fun and laughter creating and compiling this book and we really appreciate you for reading our book.

If you could possibly let us know what you thought of our book by way of a review we would really appreciate it 😊

To see all our latest books or leave a review just go to
kidsjokebooks.com
Once again, thanks so much for reading.

All the best,
Jimmy Jones
And also Ella & Alex (the kids)
And even Obi (the dog – he's very cute!)

Printed in Great Britain
by Amazon